LIL NAS X
C is for COUNTRY

illustrations by
Theodore Taylor III

Random House
New York

A is for adventure.
Every day is a brand-new start!

B is for boots—
whether they're
big or small, short or tall.

C is for country.

D is for dirt.
Mama says it's good to get down
and play in the mud!

E is for everybody.
We can all share the shine.

G is for guitar.
And music is for everyone.

H is for hat.
Look at mine—it's the tallest one I could find!

I is for
itty-bitty pony.

J is for joy.

Nothing makes me happier than a ride with Panini.

K is for kingdom.
And this here? This is mine.

L is for lullaby.

N is for nap time.

O is for Old Town Road.
This road is the prettiest one to ride on.

P is for Panini.
Night night, little pony.

Q is for quality time with family.
Don't forget the meatballs and spaghetti,
garlic bread, and Mama's desserts.

R is for rodeo.

S is for swag.
Just 'cause I'm going to bed doesn't mean I can't look good!

T is for thankful.
I love my fam!

U is for up.
Every night, I love looking up
and seeing all the stars.

W is for wagon.

X is for eXtra.
Just like me, they want to be all dressed up, even for bed.

Y is for y'all.

We've got love for everybody, no matter who you are,
where you're from, what you look like.

Z is for . . . zzzzz.

For my nieces and nephews growing up in this crazy world.
You are capable of all things and powerful beyond measure.
Never stop going after what you want. ♥
—L.N.X.

To my wife and son, Sarah and Theo,
for your love, support, and motivation
—T.T.

NIGHT NIGHT!

All rights reserved. Published in the United States by Random House Children's Books, a division of Penguin Random House LLC, New York.

Random House and the colophon are registered trademarks of Penguin Random House LLC.

Visit us on the Web! rhcbooks.com

Educators and librarians, for a variety of teaching tools, visit us at RHTeachersLibrarians.com

Library of Congress Cataloging-in-Publication Data
Names: Lil Nas X, author. | Taylor, Theodore, III, illustrator.
Title: C is for country / Lil Nas X ; illustrated by Theodore Taylor III.
Description: First edition. | New York : Random House, 2021. | Summary: "An illustrated ABC book that makes children from all
parts of America feel that they belong and can be their true selves" —Provided by publisher.
Identifiers: LCCN 2020020679 (print) | LCCN 2020020680 (ebook) | ISBN 978-0-593-30078-7 (hardcover) | ISBN 978-0-593-30079-4 (library binding) | ISBN 978-0-593-30080-0 (epub)
Subjects: LCSH: Lil Nas X, 1999-—Juvenile literature. | Alphabet books. | CYAC: Lil Nas X, 1999- | Alphabet. | LCGFT: Alphabet books.
Classification: LCC ML3930.L465 L55 2021 (print) | LCC ML3930.L465 (ebook) | DDC 421/.1—dc23

The artist used Procreate to create the illustrations for this book.
Book design by Nicole de las Heras

MANUFACTURED IN CHINA   10 9 8 7 6 5 4 3 2   First Edition

Random House Children's Books supports the First Amendment and celebrates the right to read.